,

:t

Reading to children ~~~~~~~~ ~ute to their early success in school. By the time your child enters Kindergarten, you may have read <u>more than</u> 1000 books together! This book is a gift and a reminder of the value of establishing book-sharing routines. We hope this book may become one of many books in your home library or that you will consider recycling it, and others you wish to donate, through your neighbourhood school.

Our project operates in partnership with Saanich School District. In this past year, our work was supported by the Peninsula Chapter of 100+ Women Who Care, Peninsula Co-op Food Centre, ORCA Book Publishers, Times Colonist Literacy Society, Golf for Kids, Saanich Peninsula Literacy, Butchart Gardens, the Districts of North and Central Saanich, and Beacon Books; as well as individuals, service clubs, and many family-serving agencies on the Saanich Peninsula.

Victory at Paradise Hill

Victory at Paradise Hill

written and illustrated by William Roy Brownridge

ORCA BOOK PUBLISHERS

We had won. A month ago we had won the final game and the North Line Cup along with it. Anita, Petou and I basked in the glow of victory.

I had played in goal despite a crippled foot. Anita, the only girl in the league, had made a key save. And Petou, smallest player of all, had scored the winning goal.

I dreamed that game again and again, in my sleep and waking too.

Then my dream melted. One morning I looked outside and groaned. A quick trip to the rink told a sad story. Our ice was a pool of slush. Mother Nature whispered in spring's warm, wet voice, "Sorry. No more hockey this year."

I was restless all through the windy spring and into the hot holidays of summer. With my bad foot, I couldn't play the summer games.

Instead, I read book after book and picked up a pencil and a paintbrush.

Aching for the next hockey season, I read hockey books and drew hockey scenes. I sent my favorite drawing to my brother Bob, who lived in Toronto and played for the Maple Leafs.

Bob wrote back, "Your drawing's hanging by my bed, Danny. You've got real talent!" Those words were special, even more special than the hockey stick that came with them, signed by every guy who played for the Leafs.

I rode through the rest of that summer on a wave, drawing hockey, hockey, hockey.

October brought cutting winds and steel-gray skies. Snow fell. Eager, I watched ice edge in around the rims of the sloughs. One Sunday morning the phone rang.

"Danny, hurry! Weber's Slough is frozen solid." Petou's voice was tinny, breathless.

Bingo burst out the door with me, his barks ringing in the clear, cold air.

Our first taste of hockey in five months. We played until dark, Anita, Petou and I, along with our teammates from the Wolves.

Then, bubbling with talk of the new season, we headed home.

Halfway back, Coach Matteau met us. He looked stern. And sad.

"Bad news, kids. The league has ruled that Danny and Anita can't play anymore. Petou, you can try out next week. Anita, Danny, I wish things were different."

Our hopes, crushed in a few words.

Next morning I buried myself in my blankets. That afternoon I wrote to Bob, my words big and black on the white paper.

Weeks rolled by. Winter blew into town full force, but I saw nothing to smile about. Then some good news came along. Or so I thought.

"Bob called. He's coming home for Christmas," Dad said one night at dinner.

A few days later, we waited in the wind for the Greyhound to roar into town. The door opened with a grunt and a hiss.

I was bursting to tell Bob my problems, but he was tired.

"You can talk tomorrow. Let Bob rest," Dad said.

It was a strange homecoming. No talking, no laughing. Just quiet.

The next day started off better. We decorated our tree. Anita and Petou came over to help and so did Bob's friend, Chuck.

"Bob," Chuck said when we were all sitting around the tree sipping hot chocolate, "our team's playing in the Paradise Hill tournament tomorrow. We sure could use your help on the forward line."

Bob looked at the floor. "I don't know, Chuck. Tomorrow's Christmas Eve."

"Maybe you're right, son," Dad said. "Why don't you stay home so we can have a chance to visit?"

I stared. Dad was Bob's biggest fan. He had never suggested that Bob NOT play hockey before.

"I know," Chuck said to Dad. "Come watch him play! We've got room. Danny, Petou, Anita, you too. And Bingo. Why not?" That seemed to settle it. Bob smiled, finally. With a quick look at Dad, he agreed to go.

But Mom and Dad stayed home.

Watching Bob skate for the Wildcats was fantastic, but for some reason he didn't play a lot. Even so, he was in the thick of things from the bench, cheering and shouting tips. Our team won its first two games by scores of six to three and four to one.

    The championship game was tied two to two late in the third period, headed for overtime. In the final minute Bob jumped on the ice for one last shift. He took a pass at center ice, skated around the defenseman and fired a slick wrist shot to the top left corner . . . the winning goal!

The final whistle blew and the Wildcats went crazy. Bob was swarmed by his teammates. We three kids were hoarse from screaming. Even Bingo barked excitedly.

But Bob didn't seem happy at all. He was first off the ice, gathering up his equipment and heading straight for Chuck's old car. Chuck, who'd pulled a muscle in the final, limped after him.

The rest of the team was off to the local hotel to celebrate, but we started for home.

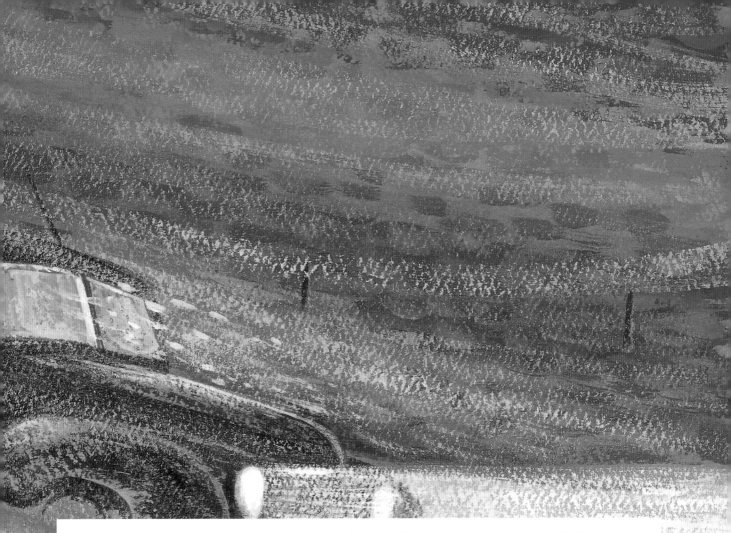

We hadn't gone far when we realized that we were in trouble. Snow whipped across the road in great white gusts. Drifts built fast. Bob held the engine at full throttle and geared down again and again.

Bang! The car lurched, swerved and plowed into the snow-filled ditch.

"Gears are gone," Chuck said. I swallowed hard.

Bob got out to see where we were. I crawled over Petou and slipped out the door behind him.

In both directions, a long line of fading fence posts and telephone poles was all we could see through the swirling snow. At least at first.

"Hey," I shouted, grabbing Bob's arm and pointing. "There's Picnic Lake! LaClares' farm is down that shore." He didn't answer. Just bundled us back into the car.

"You could skate," I said. "You could skate for help. The wind is blowing the ice clear."

"I don't think I can skate anymore," Bob said finally, his voice muffled. "That's why I came home. I'm off the Leafs. My knees are shot. Dad didn't want me to skate today. And he was right."

We were all quiet after that.

Then, "You have to go," I said. "No one's coming along this road tonight. And no one else in this car can do it."

Bob nodded slowly. He laced on his skates and opened the door.

I gave Bingo a shove. "Go with him, Bingo. Keep him safe."

I was scared, really scared. Bob's knees were shot and he was out there in the cold. If anything happened to my brother today, I would be to blame.

The engine stopped and the heater with it. No more gas. We tried to cheer each other up by singing, but our sad chorus was drowned out by the wind. I was more tired than I had ever been. Propping my eyes open with my fingers, I snuggled up against Anita and Petou.

Was I dreaming or awake when the faint tinkle of sleigh bells reached my ears?

I woke up in a hospital bed. Mom and Dad were there, but where was Bob? Where was Bingo? And Anita and Petou? I tried to sit, but fell back. My skin burned.

"Take it easy, kiddo," Dad said.

"But Bob," I croaked, "and Bingo?"

"They made it," Dad said. "Bob won't be going anywhere for a few days, but he got to the LaClares'. Bingo too."

Mom's hand was cool on my hot skin.

"Bob's in the next bed, fast asleep. You sleep too, son," she said, and I did.

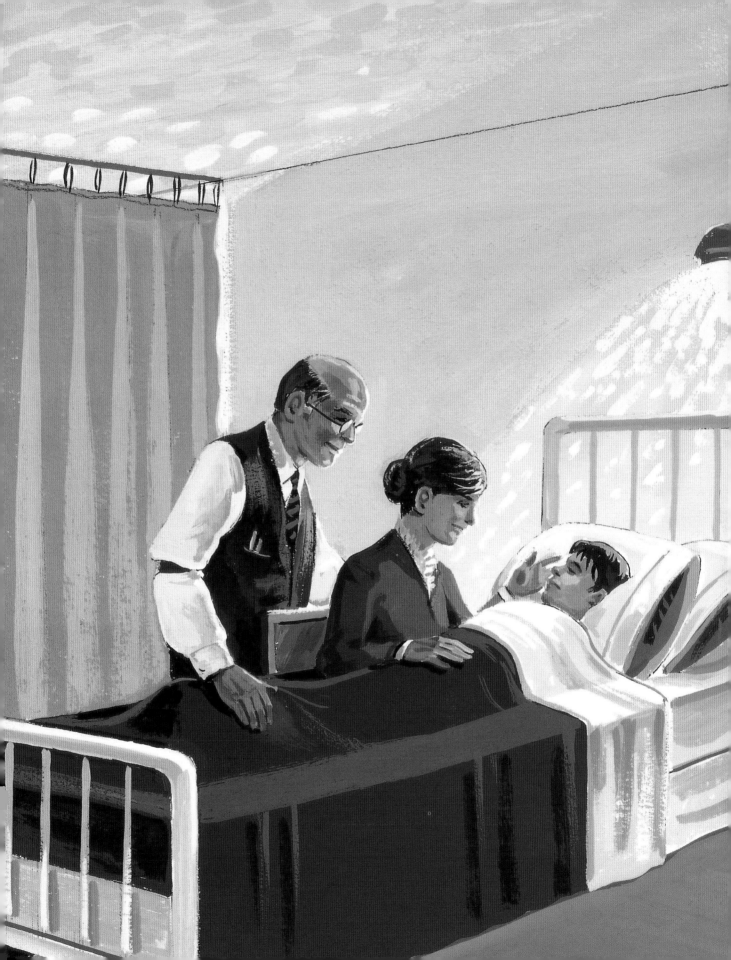

We celebrated Christmas right there in the Paradise Hill hospital room, Anita's, Petou's and Chuck's families too.

My present for Bob was a painting, one of the best I'd ever done. In it Bob looked strong and tough. Bob looked at me and smiled, a small, lopsided smile, nothing like the grin in my picture. We both knew that he was never going to be the hockey player in the picture again. His gift to me was paint, a row of fat silver tubes in a slim wooden box, exotic-sounding colors — Payne's gray, alizarin crimson and ultramarine blue.

Later that night he told me what had happened out there on Picnic Lake.

"Bingo saved us," he said. "I was ready to lie down on that ice, but he wouldn't let me. And then, right at the LaClares' fence, I hit the ground. He ran to their door barking and barking. Bingo saved all of us."

After that, not being able to skate bothered me a lot less . . . at least a lot less than it did Bob. After all, I was still the moccasin goalie in our regular pickup games. And I could draw and paint. It seemed that all Bob did was sleep and sit in Dad's big chair, listening to the radio.

I did a lot of thinking through the rest of that Christmas holiday.

The last morning dawned clear and windless. The rink would be a perfect sheet of ice.

I was almost out the door, stick in hand, when an image of Bob at the Paradise Hill tournament came to me, not scoring the winning goal, but shouting tips from the bench. How excited he had looked!

"Hey, Bob," I called up to his room. "We're heading out to the rink. Want to come and show us some moves? Tell us how it's done?"

For a moment I waited in the early morning quiet of the hallway. Then my brother appeared at the top of the stairs, grinning down at me in his pajamas.

Not Bob the hockey player, Bob the coach.

To my parents, Theresa Vivian Cochlan and Roy Harper Brownridge,
who always gave unconditional love to their child.
WB

National Library of Canada Cataloguing in Publication Data

Brownridge, William Roy, 1932-

Victory at Paradise Hill

ISBN 1-55143-219-6

I. Title.

PS8553.R694V52 2002   jC813'.54   C2002-910459-9

PZ7.B8242Vi 2002

First published in the United States, 2002

Library of Congress Control Number: 2002104411

Summary: Sequel to *The Moccasin Goalie* and *The Final Game*. When Danny's brother Bob can no longer play
hockey and Danny himself is not allowed to try out for the local team, the two find ways to help each other move on.

Teacher's guide available from Orca Book Publishers.

Orca Book Publishers gratefully acknowledges the support of its
publishing programs provided by the following agencies: the Department
of Canadian Heritage, the Canada Council for the Arts, and the
British Columbia Arts Council.

Design by Christine Toller
Printed and bound in Hong Kong

IN CANADA: IN THE UNITED STATES:
Orca Book Publishers   Orca Book Publishers
PO Box 5626, Station B   PO Box 468
Victoria, BC Canada   Custer, WA   USA
V8R 6S4   98240-0468

04 03 02 • 5 4 3 2 1